13

THE WONDERF[UL] WORLD OF WORDS

The Queen Goes to the Rescue

Dr Lubna Alsagoff
PhD (Stanford)

Marshall Cavendish
Children

The queen had a
good friend who lived
in a lovely cottage
in a quiet grove next
to WOW Forest.

The queen was very worried when she received a letter from her friend.

Madam Madevline Modal
Grove Cottage
WOW

Dear Veronica,

I need your help urgently. I seem to have lost my memory. I cannot remember the past. Please come as soon as you can. When you arrive, you will know what I mean.

Love,
Maddy

The queen immediately packed a small overnight bag.

She hopped into her car and made her way to her friend's cottage.

It was quite late by the
time the queen arrived
at her friend's home.

Yes, but let's get you inside first. We'll have dinner and an early night. And we can begin tomorrow.

Maddy kept a diary to remember what she did.

I clean the windows yesterday.

I dust the cupboards yesterday.

I plant some flowers yesterday.

I walk the dog yesterday.

I mail some letters.

10

The queen noticed that something was missing from Maddy's verbs when she was talking about the past.

The queen immediately pulled out some verb endings from her pocket.

If you want to talk about things in the past, you have to add an **ed** ending to your verbs.

I cleaned the windows yesterday.

I dusted the cupboards yesterday.

I planted some flowers yesterday.

I walked the dog yesterday.

I mailed some letters.

To make the past tense for regular verbs, add **ed**.

Present Tense	Past Tense
climb	climbed
help	helped
jump	jumped
kiss	_____
land	_____
peel	_____

You must remember to spell the past tense forms correctly!

If a verb ends in **e**, you only add **d**.

dance ➡ danced

like ➡ liked

agree ➡ agreed

If a verb has a short vowel and ends in a consonant, you need to double the consonant and add **ed**.

stop ➡ stopped

plan ➡ planned

If a verb ends in a consonant and y,
you change the y to an i then add ed.

tidy ➡ tidied

carry ➡ carried

But if the word ends in a vowel and y, you add ed.

play ➡ played

enjoy ➡ enjoyed

Irregular verbs change to a completely different form
for the past tense.

Present Tense	Past Tense
is	was
have	had
do	_____
come	_____
drive	drove
feed	fed
fly	_____
freeze	_____
go	went
swim	swam
sleep	_____

Maddy was very happy to have all her past tense endings back. She wrote in her diary.

Dear Diary,

Last week, Veronica _____ [amec] to visit me. It _____ [swa] so nice that she _____ [otko] time out of her busy schedule and _____ [vodre] all the way here.

I _____ [dha] a lovely time with her.
We _____ [newt] for long walks together,
and we _____ [kladet] for many hours
about the wonderful things we _____ [idd]
when we _____ [reew] in school together.

And most importantly, Veronica _____
[epdhel] me to fix all my past tense endings!

The Fabulous Forest of WOW

CLINIC

All the animals in the Forest of WOW were getting better.

Donkey did not hiccup so much.

Giraffe no longer had missing *ing*.

Monkey did not mix up his words.

And Boar's verbs now had *ed* endings!

They continued to go to the WOW Clinic to learn and practise grammar.

Boar really liked going to practise his past tense endings. Owl was a good teacher.

Owl taught Boar the different ways to make past tense verbs.

I'll say the present tense form of a verb, and you say the past tense form.

lick	licked
wash	_____
fold	_____
clean	_____
pull	_____
stretch	_____

That's very good, Boar!

Now let's try something a little harder.

Sure, Owl! I'm always keen on learning more about the past tense!

buy

buyed

The past tense of *buy* is bought.

leave

leaved

The past tense of *leave* is left.

Owl explained that there were verbs that did not take regular **ed** endings, and that Boar had to remember how to make the past tense of these irregular verbs.

Regular verbs follow rules.

Present tense verb + *ed* → past tense

paint	→ painted	spray	→	sprayed
help	→ helped	train	→	trained
need	→ needed	work	→	worked

Some regular verbs need to be spelt differently from their past tense:

imagine	→ imagined	tap	→ tapped
wipe	→ wiped	dry	→ dried
hug	→ hugged	try	→ tried

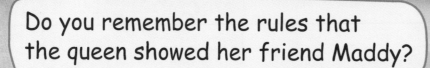

Do you remember the rules that the queen showed her friend Maddy?

20

Irregular verbs don't follow rules.
The present and past tense verbs are different.

buy → bought   sleep → slept

fly → flew   spin → spun

leave → left   think → thought

run → ran   write → wrote

There are some verbs that look the
same whether they are present or past tense.

cut → cut   put → put

hurt → hurt   shut → shut

And then there's one verb which looks the same
but is pronounced differently from its past tense.

read → read
(rhymes with reed)   (rhymes with red)

Boar loved to use the past tense. With it, he could tell his friends what he did.

Let me tell you about the wonderful things I did yesterday.

Help Boar put the past tense forms of the verbs in the right places.

are | begin | cover | dig | discover | feel | follow | go | have | jump | look | roll | scratch | start | use

I _____ for a walk in the forest yesterday.

Suddenly, a swarm of insects _____ to bite me.

So I _____ on the forest floor and _____ myself in dirt to protect myself from insects!

Then I _____ into a pond and _____ a wonderful bath!

My stomach _____ rumbling! I _____ very hungry so I _____ for some food.

I _____ my nose and _____ some plants growing by the water.

I _____ at the ground with my hoofs and _____ my tusks and _____ out some sweet potatoes!

They _____ so sweet and delicious!

Dear Parents,

In this volume, we learn about the past tense and how it helps us tell about things that happened in the past. There are some rules that we can learn, but there are many irregular past tense forms that the children need to remember.

Page	Possible Answers
12	kiss → kissed land → landed peel → peeled
13	do → did come → came fly → flew freeze → froze sleep → slept
14	came | was | took | drove
15	had | went | talked | did | were | helped
18	washed | folded | cleaned | pulled | stretched
21–22	went | began/started | rolled | covered | jumped | had | began/started | felt | looked | followed | discovered | scratched | used | dug | were

CERTIFICATE OF ACHIEVEMENT

Volume 13

Awarded to

Name _____

for mastering Volume 13

Date _____

Welcome to the **Wonderful World of Words (WOW)**!

This series of books aims to help children learn English grammar in a fun and meaningful way through stories.

Children will read and discover how the people and animals of WOW learn the importance of grammar, as the adventure unfolds from volume to volume.

What's Inside

Imaginative stories that engage children, and help develop an interest in learning grammar	Adventures that encourage children to learn and understand grammar, and not just memorise rules	Games and activities to reinforce learning and check for understanding

About the Author

Dr Lubna Alsagoff is a language educator who is especially known for her work in improving the teaching of grammar in schools and in teacher education. She was Head of English Language and Literature at the National Institute of Education (NIE), and has published a number of grammar resources used by teachers and students. She has a PhD in Linguistics from Stanford University, USA, and has been teaching and researching English grammar for over 30 years.

Published by Marshall Cavendish Children
An imprint of Marshall Cavendish International

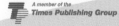
A member of the
Times Publishing Group

Printed in Singapore

visit our website at:
www.marshallcavendish.com

Marshall Cavendish
Children

CHILDREN
ISBN 978-981-5009-02-6
9 789815 009026